P9-CPZ-862

Me and You

Janet A. Holmes and Judith Rossell

NorthSouth
New York / London

To my beautiful Brenton –
my soul-mate,
husband, and friend. JAH

For my god-daughter Caitlin. JR

Text copyright © 2008 by Janet A. Holmes. Illustrations copyright © 2008 by Judith Rossell.

First published in Australia in 2008 by Little Hare Books, Surry Hills, NSW 2010 Australia, under the title *Me and You*.

First published in the United States and Canada in 2009 by North-South Books Inc.,
an imprint of NordSüd Verlag AG, CH-8005 Zürich, Switzerland.

Distributed in the United States by North-South Books Inc., New York 10001.

Library of Congress Cataloging-in-Publication Data is available.

ISBN: 978-0-7358-2250-4 (trade edition).

2   4   6   8   10   ♡   9   7   5   3   1

Printed in China.

www.northsouth.com

There are many things
that I like about being me.

I can sit quite still...

or hop,

skip

and jump.

I can stand on
my hands...

or turn somersaults.

I can float on my back...

or swim like a fish.

I can romp in the sun...

or rest in the shade.

I can build sand castles...

or dig deep holes.

I can ride up a hill...

or roll down a slope.

I can run with a kite...

or
climb
up
a
tree.

I can blow up balloons...

or burst bubbles in the bath.

I can reach
to the sky...

or curl up like a ball.

But the
thing I like
best about
being me...

is that I can be...

with you.